Daddy's Little Star

AuthorHouse™ UK
1663 Liberty Drive
Bloomington, IN 47403 USA
www.authorhouse.co.uk
UK TFN: 0800 0148641 (Toll Free inside the UK)
UK Local: 02036 956322 (+44 20 3695 6322 from outside the UK)

Because of the dynamic nature of the Internet, any web addresses or links contained in this book may have changed
since publication and may no longer be valid. The views expressed in this work are solely those of the author and do
not necessarily reflect the views of the publisher, and the publisher hereby disclaims any responsibility for them.

This book is printed on acid-free paper.

ISBN: 978-1-5246-8096-1 (sc)
ISBN: 978-1-5246-8097-8 (e)

Print information available on the last page.

Published by AuthorHouse 03/26/2022

authorHOUSE®

Daddy's Little Star

by Grace Frimpong

This book belongs to:

_____

It was a Tuesday night, and the moon was bright,
it was dark and cool, at Almond zoo.

The animals were tired, from working as if hired,
it was time to retire, a break was required.

With every mouth fed, it was off to bed,
they were heading down west, they were going to rest.

Millie was jumpy, which made her grumpy,
she didn't want to sleep, like these mummy sheep.

So, she sat on her mat, feeling sad and mad,
putting on her red boots, she left in a scoot.

On her favourite tree, where she felt very free,
she wished she could fly, like a star in the sky.

Come Wednesday morning, with a yawn as if dawn,
the animals came late, to the Lion's gate.

As Leon the lion, leaned in on his staff,
he gave out a laugh, saying, "remember to bath."

His announcement was clear without any fear,
Francesca the flamingo, is coming tomorrow.

GATEKEEPER'S LOO

Francesca

In the middle of the zoo, near the gatekeeper's loo,
in busy little hubs, the posters went up.

With writings in bold and shiny gold,
the animals were told, Francesca's not old.

Francesca the star, is coming from afar,
for the next whole day, she will be following our ways.

Curious in manner, Millie stared at the banner.
The longer she looked, the fonder she grew.

"Will she fly from the sky, and be tiny and shiny,
or twinkle with a dimple, and fall like a ball?

Will she come in a coat, on a boat that floats,
or a dome from her home, like a red and blue gnome?"

8

"Oh no," said daddy, Millie looked unhappy,
"she's famous like Amos, the albatross we crossed.

She is called a star, and celebrated afar,
for her flamingo flair, that brightens the air."

To correct her muddle, daddy gave her a cuddle,
"oh what a kerfuffle, glad you're no longer baffled."

After drinking their soup, the animals were grouped,
with dusters in clusters, doing chores in fours:
the tables and stables, the pen and the den,
the pests from the nest, and the poo in the zoo.

It was a non-stop job, without any slobs,
they worked till they dropped, and at bedtime they flopped.

Early the next day, Millie woke but never spoke,
she sneaked to a peak, looking quaint with her paint.

To be like her star, Millie opened the jar.
She was covered in ink and looked very pink.

As the animals awakened, remembering what was spoken,
they ran for the update, standing near the Lion's gate.

Millie started her walk, but was stopped at a fork;
"oink, oink," said Mr Pig, "why are you, so very pink?"

"Nevermind, Mr Pig, why I look so very pink,
I'm a mastermind you'll find, from behind, I'm looking fine."

As she shuffled along, while singing her song;
"buzz, buzz," said Mrs Bee, "why are you, so very pink?"

"Nevermind, Mrs Bee, why I look so very pink,
I'm a mastermind you'll find, from behind, I'm looking fine."

With her hand in the air, Millie brushed through her hair.
"Click, click," said baby Hare, "why are you, so very pink?"

"Nevermind, baby Hare, why I look so very pink,
I'm a mastermind you'll find, from behind, I'm looking fine."

As she neared the many rocks, she saw faces in a shock.
"Keow, keow," said the Peacocks "why are you, so very pink?"

"Nevermind, Peacocks, why I look so very pink,
I'm a mastermind you'll find, from behind, I'm looking fine."

Now near Leon's gate, Millie's mates saw her state.
So they risked their fate and missed the update.

"Quack, quack", said the duckling, "hee-haw" said the foal,
"moo, moo" said the calf and together they cried
"you look offkey, unlike a monkey,
oh Millie, this is silly. Why are you, so very pink?"

They gave Millie a pat, while sitting for their chat,
it's all too much trouble, just to look like a double.

In her royal gown without her crown,
looking down in a frown, Millie felt like a clown.

She had dressed to impress, but it turned out a mess.

As daddy came by, Millie's friends said goodbye.
"Let's rethink the pink," daddy said with a wink.

"I prefer it as ink, and not on your skin.
Just look deep within, being you is a win."

"You are a star with your own glory,
so take territory to tell your own story.

You can never be Francesca, the flamingo star,
but even better as Millie, you are daddy's little star."

Daddy's Little Star:

By Grace Frimpong

One star is different from another in glory, like the moon and the sun,
you must tell your own story.

Printed in the United States
by Baker & Taylor Publisher Services